Chicken Nuggets

Written and Illustrated by
Carol Kohring

AuthorHouse™
1663 Liberty Drive
Bloomington, IN 47403
www.authorhouse.com
Phone: 833-262-8899

Because of the dynamic nature of the Internet, any web addresses or links contained in this book may have changed since publication and may no longer be valid. The views expressed in this work are solely those of the author and do not necessarily reflect the views of the publisher, and the publisher hereby disclaims any responsibility for them.

Any people depicted in stock imagery provided by Getty Images are models, and such images are being used for illustrative purposes only.
Certain stock imagery © Getty Images.

This book is printed on acid-free paper.

ISBN: 978-1-6655-4157-2 (sc)
ISBN: 978-1-6655-4156-5 (e)

Library of Congress Control Number: 2021921458

Print information available on the last page.

Published by AuthorHouse 02/07/2022

authorHOUSE®

Dedication

This is for my husband, children, and grandchildren. I would especially like to thank Linda Meyers Wilson and Justin Marra who helped make this book possible.

Chicken nuggets to-day.
Chicken nuggets to-day.
Let's get in line, one at a time,
for chicken nuggets to-day.

Chicken nuggets to-day.
A nugg for me, a nugg for you.
There are mashed potatoes too.

Let's climb in line,
one at a time,
for chicken nuggets to-day.

Chicken nuggets to-day.
How many nuggets do you see?
Oh, I think there's more than three.

Let's ~~fart~~ fall in line
One at a time,
for chicken nuggets to-day.

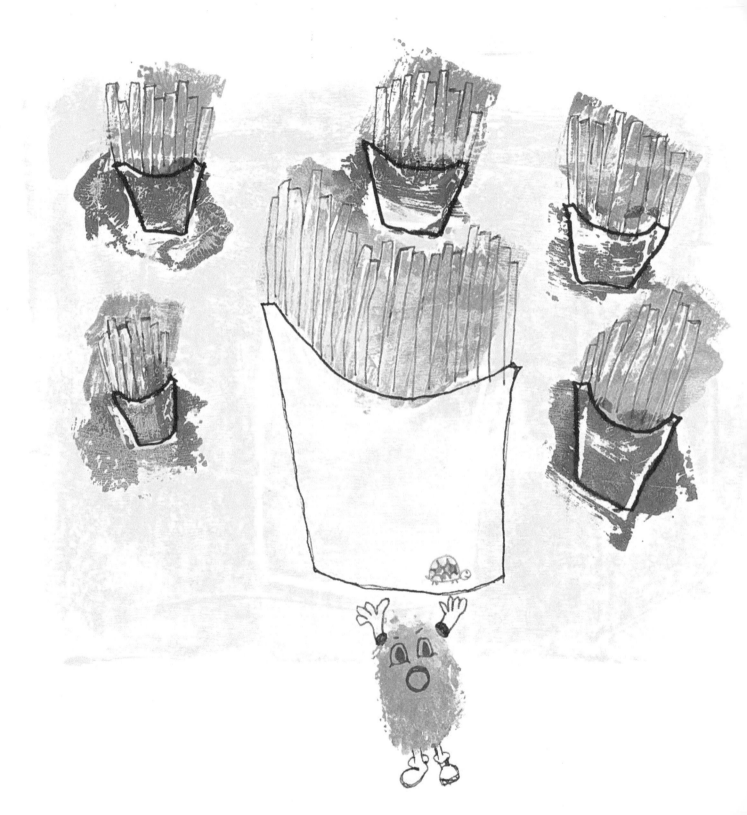

Chicken nuggets to-day.
Sometimes nuggets come with fries.
It's always nice to be surprised.

Let's jump in line,
one at a time,
for chicken nuggets to-day.

Chicken nuggets to-day.
Would you like a dipping sauce?
Dipping sauces are for free.
No, they do not grow on trees.

Let's fly in line.
One at a time,
for chicken nuggets to-day.

Chicken nuggets to-day.
Let's dip the nuggs, oh what a treat.
Then relax and eat, our day's complete.

So ride in line,
one at a time,
for chicken nuggets to-day.

Chicken nuggets to-day.
It's my favorite day.
My tummy's saying,
Yummy, Yummy it can't wait.

So join the line,
One at a time,
for chicken nuggets to-day .

It's a chickenlicious goodbye y'all.

The End!

CPSIA information can be obtained
at www.ICGtesting.com
Printed in the USA
BVHW022353250522
638001BV00006B/25

9 781665 541572